AR Quiz# 41407
BL: 5.6
AR Pts: 3.0

THROWING SMOKE

BRUCE BROOKS

THROWING SMOKE

A LAURA GERINGER BOOK
An Imprint of HarperCollins*Publishers*

Library of Congress Cataloging-in-Publication Data
Brooks, Bruce.
    Throwing smoke / by Bruce Brooks.
        p.   cm.
    Summary: When his teammates on the Breadhurst Newts baseball team continue their
losing ways, Whiz uses an unusual printing press to create several star players in hopes of
winning a game.
    ISBN 0-06-028972-4 — ISBN 0-06-028320-3 (lib. bdg.)
    [1. Baseball—Fiction.   2. Supernatural—Fiction.]   I. Title.
PZ7.B7913 Bq   2000   00-59555
[Fic]—dc21   CIP
                                                                                  AC

Typography by Alicia Mikles
1   2   3   4   5   6   7   8   9   10
❖
First Edition

For Stan Reed

The bumpy, tufty patch of ground where the Breadhurst Newts played was defined as a baseball field only because someone at the small school, many years ago, had built a rickety backstop at one corner. Even calling the backstop's place a "corner" implied too much geometry. The field covered an irregular oval space with wavy edges. Barney, the Newts' center fielder, had once observed that the shape was exactly what you might get when you cracked an egg onto a hot skillet.

Two boys came over a hummock in what would be deepest right field. One was fairly tall, with hair that looked like pine shavings. He swept the field quickly with green eyes and drew his brows together with a frown.

"Where is everybody?" he asked. "I don't like this."

"Well, at least the field's still here," said the other boy. He was short, thickly built, with long dark hair and black-framed spectacles. He too looked the field over, but his cheerful expression did not change. "Don't sweat it, Whiz. The team will show."

The boy called Whiz seemed to relax a bit, but the worry didn't leave his face. He sighed. "They've got plenty of reasons *not* to come back for another season."

"And only one reason to come. Fortunately, that one reason is *baseball*."

The stocky boy—called E6—grinned and

pointed; over the far hill that bordered the first-base line, four more kids moved into view.

Whiz narrowed his eyes. "Are they trudging, E? I do believe they are *trudging.*"

E6 squinted, shading his eyes with one hand. "No way, Captain. In fact, I see evidence of a certain, well, *dignity* in their strides, an *assured* kind of pace—"

"I wonder where they bought the dignity," said Whiz. "They sure didn't get it from our performance last year."

E6 maintained a respectful, funereal silence, fixing his eyes on an especially nasty clump of dry, hard bumps in short center field. The joke around the league was that this field, with all its scruffy irregularities, was exactly suited to the play of last year's woeful debut of the Breadhurst Newts. The Newts had managed to pull together four girls and eight boys to form a new team in the town's otherwise snazzy Little League, with an indifferent geography teacher listed as the manager. The kids had banded together with a common spirit of rebellion: All but two of them had been cut from other teams and denied the chance to play the game they loved. Then Whiz had gotten the bright idea that they could "represent" their small private school and wedge their way into the league as a unit.

It did not take long, during that first season, for the Newts to discover that loving the game was not the same as playing it. By the time they had stacked up their fourth loss in a row by more than ten runs (with their "manager" long gone in disgust), they admitted to themselves that perhaps the coaches who had cut them had been pretty wise. The trouble was, each Newt was capable of doing one thing very well, too well to be easily tossed away. Barney could run down long drives to the alleys and glove them backhand in full stride, but he got only three singles all season.

E6 played shortstop because he had no fear facing hard-bounding grounders; however, he *handled* those grounders miserably, and racked up a record thirty-three errors in eighteen games. At the same time, he batted over .450 and led the team in RBI. As for Whiz—he was the pitcher, because he alone had the gift of being able to throw the ball into the strike zone every pitch. Too bad he threw it relatively slow, and perfectly straight, so that opposing batters drooled waiting for his pitches to arrive, then whacked them to the far horizons.

Phoebe, a tall girl at first base, could catch even the most errant throw from her infielders but bobbled everything that came off a bat. Dragon, in right field, lost sight of any ball hit into the sky but told *excellent* jokes that made all the losing less painful inning by inning. So it went with all of them—one talent, many holes in fundamental technique. For the most part, they had woven a pretty strong web of friendship from the strands of talent, leaving the gaps in silence.

The final record of the first-year Breadhurst Newts: 0–10. In the round-robin playoffs: 0–2 and out. All the players had secretly uttered thanks that their parents and siblings lived many miles away and had never seen them play.

Now, Whiz thought with a shudder, the second season's start was just two weeks away. True, he and E6, the unofficial captains, had talked with all ten Newts to make certain they were coming back for more, beginning with today's practice. But Whiz still felt uneasy counting on the turnout. Losing twelve games, by an average margin of about nine runs, had a way of making you go out for the track team.

"That's the spirit!" said E6. One of the players with a bat and ball had lifted an easy fly to Dragon in short right. Before the ball landed forty feet behind him, Dragon shouted something that made the others double up in laughter as he ran to retrieve the ball.

"Well, at least we seem to still be funny," Whiz said sarcastically.

"There are worse things to be when you lose a lot," said E6.

"Name two."

"Illiterate and hungry."

Whiz was silent.

The players hollered greetings as if they had not all been together in school two hours before but, rather, had not seen each other since the last game of the previous season. In addition to Dragon, Phoebe and her twin sister, Wren (third base), had come, along with a large, visibly earnest boy named Josiah. Josiah insisted he was a catcher, though in a full season he had never quite mastered the art of putting on all his equipment correctly. He couldn't hit much, either. But he had a great arm.

"Yo," said Dragon, waving to Whiz and E6,

"the first line of our defense arrives."

Making deep eye contact, Josiah shook the hands of both boys. He referred to Whiz as "Battery Mate."

"Double-A or 9-volt?" asked Dragon.

Josiah looked blank. Wren walked up and slung an arm around his shoulders. "Jose spent the winter reading baseball books," she said. "Got all the righteous terms down pat."

Phoebe held up a ball. "What's this, Jose?"

"The horsehide," Josiah said automatically.

"See?" said Wren.

Dragon raised his eyebrows, and his cap hiked up on his forehead. "Whizzer, think you will *hum* the old *horsehide* over the *platter* with sufficient *heat* this season?"

"I can carry the mail," said Whiz, smiling. "I can chuck aspirins."

"Yeah, he can *bring it*," added E6.

"Bring what?" asked Wren. "The mail?"

"No," said Josiah, as if he'd never heard any-thing so stupid. "Pitchers *carry* the mail. They *bring*—" He floundered for a couple of seconds. "They *bring*—you know—they just bring *it*."

"Ah," said Phoebe. "Everything is clear now. Thanks, Jose."

As they talked, two boys carrying gloves and wearing caps arrived at the crest of the hill that dropped away behind the backstop. The taller of the two waved; the shorter one, who held a huge lump of something inside one cheek and wore his cap backward, merely turned his head and spat onto the ground.

"Barney and Mr. Charm," said Phoebe.

"Wu," said E6, "what is that growth inside your mouth? A tumor?"

Instead of answering, Wu pulled a foil pouch from the back pocket of his baggy khakis. He opened it, revealing what looked like a tangle of dead pink flatworms, a large pinch of which he plucked out and stuffed into his mouth.

"He calls it his *chaw*," Barney explained.

"That means 'tea' in Chinese, doesn't it?" said Dragon.

"It means 'chewing tobacco' in baseball," said Josiah.

"And it means 'shredded bubble gum' in eleven-year-old," said Barney. "Can you believe it? No one in town will sell him tobacco."

Wu pouted, or perhaps it was the only expression possible because his mouth was crammed with pink matter.

"Hey," said Whiz, with what he hoped was a casual, offhand tone, "how about a little five hundred?"

"Translation: How about we start to *practice*, to do something *productive*?" said Wren. "But no thanks on the five hundred. No one wants to stand around watching you and Barney catch balls none of us can even see."

"We'll rotate," Whiz persisted. "A fifteen-pitch max per hitter."

Dragon frowned. "That sounds suspiciously like the social disease of creeping *order*. Whereas this team is definitely better off sticking to *chaos*." But he put his glove back on and trotted out to right field. The others drifted out to their positions, with Whiz pitching and Wu batting.

Before throwing the first pitch—albeit only to open a game of 500—Whiz felt a flutter of excitement. He held the ball up close to his face. "Ball," he said, trying to sound both stern and respectful, "you have to go *faster* this year when I throw you." Then he wound up and threw. Wu cracked a long, low drive up the left-field alley. Barney ran it down and took it backhand on the third bounce. The third bounce was still at head level; that ball had been *crushed*.

Wu let out a brief yelp of celebration and eagerly resumed his stance, to wait for the next fat one. On the mound, Whiz sighed and waited for the return of his ol' pal, the ball.

"Well," he told the sphere, "speed isn't everything."

Wu poled the next pitch deep to right. Dragon, looking up and carefully drifting three steps to his left, settled and pounded his glove. He was still looking up and pounding it when the ball landed twenty-five feet behind him.

"Catching isn't everything either," Whiz muttered.

E6 heard him. "Nothing is everything, Whizzer," he said cheerily.

"Let's silkscreen that on our jerseys." Whiz threw another pitch.

DELANCEY BURNETTE

BREADHURST NEWTS
SECOND BASE
BATS: R   THROWS: R
HT: 4'11" WT: 81 LBS.

Delancey is the Newts' best
infielder, gobbling up anything
hit her way—she was among
league leaders at her position
last year, making only six
errors. Fiery, always alert, a
team leader with a good word
for teammates who get down.

Most of the Newts went from their offi-
cial practice to one of two places. First
there was Dudley's Pharmacy, which had an old-
time soda fountain where you not only could get
vanilla Cokes, but could also read through *mangas* from the *non*-old-time front of the store. Then
there was the school and its dorms. You could not
get vanilla Cokes or *mangas* there, but you could
shower, sleep, talk to your buddies, write letters to
your parents asking for money, or perhaps even
catch up on some homework.

Whiz, however, headed straight for another destination. After walking long enough to leave the others behind, he found E6 at his side.

"I don't suppose you might be going some-place aboveground?" said E6.

Whiz smiled slightly. "Got some work to catch up on." He looked at his friend. "You want to come with me?"

"So you can make your ritual sacrifice to the vampires down there? You don't fool *me*, Whizzer." E6 shook his head. "That place gives me the creeps big-time. I can't understand how you put up with it."

Whiz laughed. "Easy. I'm not a wuss with too much imagination."

E6 frowned and made big gestures. "Those presses. They're so *huge*, and so *dark*, and all these things *move* when they're printing."

"That's called *work*, E," said Whiz with an-other laugh, which E6 might not have noticed was kind of forced. "You remember—energy, mass, motion, all that stuff. Mr. Dougal's shop is just a cool little place off an alley below the street, and printing is just an easy job."

E6 shook his head. "You can't fool me. You've sold your soul to the typefaces, and you're a zombie now—"

"And I'm *hungry!*" said Whiz, spinning on E6 and grabbing him. They scuffled, but afterward, Whiz resumed his path.

E6 stayed where he was. "You really going to work now?" he said.

"Got some business cards to finish before tomorrow," Whiz called over his shoulder.

E6 shook his head. "Beware the vampires."

"I'll keep my eyes open," said Whiz. "Or maybe *shut.*"

E6 was out of earshot. Whiz walked on.

BARNEY OLIVER

BREADHURST NEWTS
CENTER FIELD
BATS: L THROWS: R
HT: 5'6" WT: 105 LBS.

As long as Barney is in center, the Newts are good up the all-important middle. He's on the ball off the bat, with killer speed and a flawless eye. The heart of the team's confidence, Barney has the kind of good nature that helps everyone enjoy playing even in tough times.

To be perfectly honest, Whiz was just as glad E6 did not accompany him to the print shop. True, E6 was his best friend and often kept him company while he worked. But there were times when Whiz simply wanted to be alone in the shop. He knew how lucky he had been to get this particular job in Breadhurst's unique school-town work program. Mr. Dougal, the owner and the only other person who worked there, had given him his own key during the summer, and since then Whiz had used the print shop as a place where he could find his deepest moments of solitude.

He never knew when he might need one. He realized, after the Newts' semipractice, that he needed one now.

Alone, he descended the steps that led down from street level to the alley. He took his key and let himself into the dark printery.

He felt as he always did: He was in the presence of some kind of power, familiar but inexplicable. E6 had not been wrong. In the dimness, the great, hulking machines seemed to be holding a force in check, as if what they could print would forever be a sort of secret resolution of problems not yet dreamed of—or a threat.

Whiz switched on some lights.

Even in the light, the tall Linotypes and presses looked strong, all black iron struts and discs— the first time he'd seen them, Whiz had thought they could have been used to play the part of alien robots in those old black-and-white space movies. But once Mr. Dougal had taught him the techniques for operating them, Whiz had pretty much fallen in love with the robots. He had fallen in love with printing.

Before he went to the business-card job, Whiz pulled a bunch of large printed cards from a secret place behind a Linotype machine. These were printed on a special, thick stock; their layout was bold and elegant.

Whiz flipped through the cards, pulling out this one or that for a quick reading. Of course, he knew every word on the cards—he had written all the facts, descriptions, and statistics before laying them out and printing them. The cards comforted Whiz in a way he couldn't explain to himself, much less to anyone else, which was why the set was his secret. When he read the card about, say, Barney, the fact that there existed a Barney created entirely by *words* made the experience of seeing the real Barney seem doubly genuine *and* doubly magical. Sometimes, when Whiz encountered one of the players in the flesh soon after reading his or her card, he let himself feel for a moment that the words had created a player to match them. He knew it was pretty goofy to do this, but it gave him a strange kick.

Carefully, he put the cards back into their hiding place and turned his attention to the regular work he needed to do. Soon, something familiar but mysterious happened to him: He went into a kind of working trance, something E6, who had watched it plenty of times from his stool in the corner, called *the ink zone-out.* His blood seemed to tap its way through his body with the exact rhythm of the press's cycle of impression. His hands darted toward the pins with blank cards and darted away with printed ones, and he never had a thought. The grind of the rollers, the clink of the platen rotating on its iron gear—he did not so much *hear* these sounds as take them deep into himself.

E6 said it best: "You're just another part of the press, man. You may be weird, but you fit smoothly."

On the day of the Newts' first practice, Whiz was so deep in "the ink zone" that he did not notice the sound of the printery's front door opening and closing. It was not until a moving shape caught the corner of his eye in the pressroom that he realized E6 had decided to follow him after all.

"Another Stone Age masterpiece completed," said E6, walking up to the press and picking up one of the cards by its edges. He knew enough not to smear the wet ink. He read aloud, "*Bart's Parts, Automotive Supplies—'Nothing's Junk to Us!'*"

"Obviously, Bart hasn't seen our baseball team," said Whiz, turning off the press.

E6 flipped the card back onto the pile. "Hey,

go back into the zone if you're going to keep cranking on the Newts. What's with all of these"—he put his fingers on his temples and frowned—"these *negative waves,* man?"

Whiz was scrubbing his hands with a rag that used to be red. "Got to face the facts, that's all."

"The *facts,*" said E6, slipping onto his stool, "consist of: One, the new season has yet to begin, and Two, our players have yet to show how much they have improved."

"Improved? Improved their baseball skills over the winter, while playing basketball and ice hockey?"

"Improved their *athletic* skills in general," said E6, a bit defensively.

"Baseball players are not just 'athletes,'" said Whiz, throwing the rag into a large metal bin. "They need very refined abilities."

"Oooh, getting dainty, are we?" said the short-stop. "Well, maybe some of us have even gotten more *refined* since last year. I, for example, now follow through on my throws to first with my pinky bent, as if I were drinking tea with the king of England."

"England doesn't have a king," Whiz said. "And you throw for crap."

"What an opening you give me for a snappy comeback, pitcher boy. However, in the interest of team spirit, I will resist. Instead, I will improve my mind."

E6 picked up the old copy of the huge *Baseball Encyclopedia* they kept in the corner and began flipping through the pages. Whiz occupied himself by cleaning the press. After a while, studying a page, E6 said, "I wish I could have seen Frank Robinson play. Winning the MVP in consecutive years, once in *each league*—wow."

Without looking up from his scrubbing, Whiz said, "We're too late even to see him *manage*. He had the Orioles while we were playing with rattles and stuffed bears."

"*You* were probably playing with kitchen knives and disposable lighters."

Whiz sat on a stool and looked at E6. "Well? What do you think? About the team. The players."

E6 scratched the back of his head. "Is this, like, the general two-word summary, or a position-by-position rundown?"

"Position-by-position."

E6 thought for a moment. "That's too detailed, but I will break things down a *little*." He cleared his throat. "It's early to tell, naturally, since we only had one loose practice. But I'd say that up the middle we have severe limitations, and down the lines we are inconsistent but mostly pretty weak." He smiled.

"Golly gee," said Whiz. "Where do I sign up for this adventure in sportsmanship?"

"But I do think we'll have some fun," said E6.

"How nice," said Whiz.

E6 suddenly slapped the two huge open leaves of *The Baseball Encyclopedia* shut, making a loud *whap* that nearly toppled Whiz from his stool. The smile was still on E6's face, but when he spoke, his voice sounded serious.

"What, have you been watching too much *Mighty Ducks* junk lately or something? Started thinking we shouldn't cut *really* loose and enjoy *playing* until we win win win the big championship at the end of the movie?" He shook his head, still smiling. "What's with this attitude, all the gloom about 'skills' and stuff?"

Whiz looked as if he were caught between the urge to blast back at E6 and the need to silence the disquiet that had been rotating inside his chest since he had first started getting the team together for the second season. The defensive heat passed; he let out a big breath and gave E6 a long shrug.

"I know it's not fair, or even *enjoyable*, to pick at everyone's goofs, as if I was perfect myself, or as if perfection was even something worth looking for," he said. "But it's just—well, sometimes last year, I think I saw that losing can be so *close* to winning, it's just, like, knowing how to *take* a game because you *want* it. And to want it, to want winning, you have to have felt it and liked the feeling." He looked at E6 apologetically. "Sometimes last year, getting beat so bad—I *hated* it, I just couldn't *tolerate* it, I thought I was going to go really crazy. I know I was supposed to be 'playing,' the way you say. But to me, I was just 'losing.'"

E6 listened, then said, "So change things."

Whiz gave a bitter chuckle, then started waving his hands and wiggling his fingers. "Sure. Like, jibbida-jibbida-boo, now Barney can hit as well as he fields. And wocko-wocko-wee, I'm fast and I even have a curve."

"The last part is exactly what I mean," said E6. "Look—how much did you pitch during the winter? Were the times I caught you in the gym the only times?"

Whiz looked down and nodded.

"That was four times, about forty-five minutes each. And I don't recall you working on new pitches or anything. You just threw as usual, keeping your control, right?"

"Pretty much. Listen, without control, you—"

"I know, I know. Control's important. Plus, it's about all you've got, as a pitcher. So it's even *more* important. Okay. But the thing is—you didn't practice much over the off-season, didn't, like, acquire any new 'skills' or anything."

Whiz made a gesture of impatience. "So what's your point?"

E6 ignored the impatience. He smiled again. "Just this. I saw Wren and Phoebe playing catch for an hour almost every day through half of

November, on the lacrosse field, and they started again in March. Sometimes Delancey was there and they practiced fielding grounders."

"Okay," said Whiz. "I didn't know. That's really good, really, I'm glad to hear it."

E6 wasn't finished. "Barney and Wu and even *Dragon* did fungoes three or four times a week through the fall, at the old YMCA in town."

"Dragon?" said Whiz. "No way! You saw him today. He can't judge a fly ball any better than he could last season."

E6 nodded. "That's probably right. And now we come to the big point. What does it tell you, that Dragon practiced pretty hard but got no better?"

"All right, all right," said Whiz. "Lesson understood. 'Some people cannot improve no matter what they do.' Correct?"

"You got it," said E6. "But now you have to think about it. Until you stop twitching and moaning and studying up on how miserable the season is going to be. Some people can just play the game, Whizzer. Some people can only try. You can't turn one kind into the other."

Whiz nodded slowly. "Okay," he said with a sigh. "Fine. I'll try to stop anticipating disaster, stop noticing how crummy we all play. Okay! But—"

"What?"

Whiz looked at E6. "But while we're all being the kind of people who can only try, is it all right for me to wish we had a few of the kind who can *play*?"

"I guess," said E6 uncertainly. "As long—well, just don't let your *wishing* start feeling like *doing*. The Newts are the Newts. Daydreaming about stud hosses who throw sliders and whack taters isn't going to change us."

Whiz nodded reluctantly but said nothing.

WREN JAMES

B READHURST N EWTS
T HIRD B ASE
B ATS: R T HROWS: R
H T: 5'1" W T: 85 LBS.

Wren plays a solid "hot
corner," with great reflexes on
those scary drives up the line.
At the plate she can be counted
on to get on base—she batted
.300 last season and led the
team in bases on balls. Kind,
but with a wicked wit, she
keeps everybody honest by
speaking her mind.

4

Wren swung a little high and topped the
ball but still got enough of it to send
a smart two-hopper to Delancey at second.
Delancey, as she often told everyone, could *pick
it*, and she picked this one, clean, and fired a
throw to Phoebe at first. Whiz stood in admira-
tion. *Such a simple thing. The ball is pitched, the
ball is struck, the ball is caught, thrown, caught.
Amazing when it's done right.* His musing kept
him from seeing Phoebe's toss back to him; the
ball hit him in the chest.

"Be alive in there!" hollered Dragon from right.

"Why should we?" snapped the boy called Duke, who was standing in for Wren at third. Duke was one of the team's three bench players, largely because he could not play baseball worth a bent penny. He was a football star in the fall, and let his name be added to the Newt roster only because he thought stardom in one sport guaranteed at least competence in every other. He was incorrect.

He did not get all that many chances to prove it when he played third, however—very few of the Newts' mostly right-handed batters could pull even Whiz's pokey pitches Duke's way.

Wren grabbed her glove and trotted out to third. "Okay, big guy," she said. "Go try to stay awake with a bat in your hands."

"With *lumber* in his hands," came Josiah's correction, muffled by his mask.

"Whatever," said Wren.

On the first pitch, Duke tried to pull the ball himself, with a huge cut that sent a meek grounder to Wren, who dug it out backhanded. Her two-bounce throw to the vicinity of first beat him by ten steps, because he took the time to fling the bat hard into the ground with a curse.

"That's it," Duke said. Grabbing his glove, he stomped behind the backstop toward the hill. "I'm through with this wussy game and this bunch of losers."

"Uh-oh," said Josiah, "a *walkout*."

"No," called Dragon, "just a *chickenhearted jerk*."

Duke made a nasty gesture over his shoulder and disappeared over the edge of the hill without looking back.

"We don't need him," said Wren.

Whiz disagreed. "What if you get measles? *Hey, Duke, hold on!*"

"Let him go," said E6. "He plays baseball like a linebacker."

"But—"

"And *I* play it like a ballet dancer," said Maria, one of the two remaining benchwarmers, who was, at the moment, actually warming the bench. She didn't even have a glove to pick up as she stood and walked gracefully after Duke, nose in the air.

"Maria!" said Whiz. "Wait, you can't—"

"She *is* a ballet dancer, Whiz," said Phoebe. "Let her go."

Delancey had already run in and picked up two bats, which she whirled around a couple of times before dropping one and standing up to the plate. "Just chuck it, Whiz," she said.

"Where's Justin?" Whiz asked, looking around. "He's supposed to take your spot at second while you hit. *Hey, Justin*—"

"I forgot to tell you," said E6. "He quit."

"Quit?"

"Mannheim told him he'd lose his scholarship if he didn't raise his grades in four subjects by the end of the year. Justin decided to take on algebra first."

"Crunching the numbers."

"Shut up, Jose," said Whiz. Then to E6, "Do you realize this leaves us with—"

"—with no scrubs," said Phoebe. "So what?"

"We're all scrubs," said Whiz, "but this—"

"Leaves us with no *sub*scrubs. I repeat: So what?"

"You going to pitch or not?" said Delancey, waving the bat.

With a sigh and a shake of the head, Whiz threw the ball. Delancey swung mightily and missed. She repeated the whiff on the next five pitches but lined the sixth clean over second base into center field.

"Wow," she said, watching in a satisfied

standstill as Barney charged the ball, fielded it cleanly on first bounce, and threw a rocket to first.

"You're out, Lance," said Whiz as the ball smacked into Phoebe's mitt with a small puff of dust. "That was very professional, the way you ran it out."

She shot him a nasty look. "You want professional? Where's my paycheck?"

"Where's your pride?"

"I hit the ball, didn't I? I'm proud of *that.*"

"It's no good if you don't— Oh, never mind." Whiz scuffed off the mound. "Okay if we call this practice before anyone else quits?"

E6 protested mildly. "The first game is Saturday."

Whiz shrugged and took a drink from his water bottle. The fielders straggled in to the bench. Josiah tried to flip his mask off but caught one of the straps on his nose. Eventually he freed himself; then, acting as if nothing had happened, he said, "So, what's our game-day strategy, Whizzer?"

Dragon, after a gulp of water, said, "I say we let them get an eight-run lead by the third to dupe them into a false sense of security, and then let them slowly pull away."

"*Six* runs by the third ought to be enough. We *do* have our pride," said Delancey, glancing at Whiz.

"We beat their butts blue," said Wu.

"Absolutely," said Barney.

"Well, we do have to *try*," said Whiz. He looked around at their faces. "Right?"

"Absolutely," said Josiah.

The rest of them muttered vaguely, trying for half-spirited echoes of cheer, but sounding only like a chorus of ghosts.

"At the very least"—Whiz sighed—"we all have to show up on time. We have no substitutes."

"We'll be here," said Phoebe, smacking a fist into her mitt with another dusty puff.

"Maybe the other team won't," Dragon said hopefully.

DRAGON FLETCHER

BREADHURST NEWTS
RIGHT FIELD
BATS: R   THROWS: R
HT: 4'10" WT: 77 LBS.

Dragon is incredibly smart and
incredibly funny.

But *the other team* *did* show up. They were the Hawks, who had finished third in the league the year before and fourth in the play-offs. Their main strength back then had been the incredibly fast pitching of twin brothers named Vasquez.

But the Vasquez boys had stepped up to the next age level, and it was clear in this game that the rest of the team had not adjusted to the fact that it could no longer count on three of every four opposing batters striking out. The Hawk outfielders were slow off the bat, letting several soft Newt liners drop in for hits in the first two innings; and the Hawk infielders watched grounders coming at them as if they had never seen such a thing before.

Of course, the Hawks still got a chance to bat, and the Hawks could *hit*. With Whiz bearing down as hard as he could on every pitch, they managed only four runs by the middle of the third. When Wu yanked a home run with Wren and E6 on base in the bottom half of the inning, the Newts actually took their first lead in two years, 6–4.

Then they promptly made three errors in the top of the fourth (two by E6) and gave back two runs. But Whiz saw that the brief lead had given his teammates ideas of glory, and he did his best to keep his pitches away from the heart of the plate.

In the bottom of the inning, Dragon surprised everyone by bunting down the third-base line and beating it out. The pitcher, flustered as a Vasquez would never have been, hit Whiz on the thigh with a hard, wild pitch, and Phoebe came up with two on and nobody out.

Whiz watched from first, happy with the prospects despite his throbbing thigh. The pitcher tried unsuccessfully to throw a curve on the third pitch, hanging the ball in front of Phoebe's eyes, and she smacked it right back at the mound. It hit the pitcher sharply in the shins. He went down with a cry. The catcher and third baseman both chased the ball as it bounced across the infield. When the catcher came up with it, he had nowhere to throw—Dragon slid unnecessarily into third, Whiz stood on second, and Phoebe rounded first cautiously.

The Hawks' coach lifted the stricken pitcher to his feet, gave him a shove off the field, and waved to the bench. A very fat boy with red hair and extremely pink skin got up and plodded to the mound. He took the ball, wound up, and fired it hard over his catcher's head. When it hit the backstop with a crunching, metallic sound, Whiz shuddered; when the next five warm-up pitches did the same, he knew he was hearing bells ringing the end of the Newt rally.

"Batter up," said the umpire.

Delancey, looking terrified, swung at the first three pitches, all of which were on a level with her nose and a foot outside. One down. Barney stepped in with a fierce look on his face that Whiz knew meant only that he, like Delancey, was scared half blind. It took him *four* pitches to fan. Two gone.

"Stop the bleeding!" hollered Josiah from the bench. "No more K's! Who's up?"

"You are," Whiz yelled.

After chasing two horrible pitches with mighty cuts, Jose took a third strike—the first ball the fat kid had managed to put across the plate.

Phoebe was stomping, furious about her wasted clutch single; Dragon was limping with a strawberry from his cool slide; and Whiz felt a bruise growing on his leg, not to mention on his spirit. The rest of the Newts looked discouraged and resigned. Whiz watched them all shift readily into the old habit of thinking, *Oh, well, here it comes again.*

He was guilty himself. He started pitching politely, as if his job were to tee the ball up for the Hawk hitters. They obliged him by whacking it to all parts of the field. Except for Barney and Delancey, the defense fell to pieces. Josiah took a hard foul tip in the chest and got a little ball shy, letting three pitches get by him with men on base. Worse, as the Hawks spent their halves of the last two innings rounding the bases, the Newts failed to get another hit. Final score: 15–6.

"We had the suckers on the run," Wu steamed after throwing his cap into a tree. "You bozos had to go and strike out with the bases loaded."

"The sacks were jammed," said Josiah.

"We like *you*, too, Wu," said Delancey. "So we won't even mention the three fly balls you dropped in the last two innings."

"I hit a three-run homer, didn't I?"

"And very pretty it was, you selfish pig," said Wren. "Unfortunately, a hailstorm failed to break out just after you touched the plate, and we had to play the rest of the game. *All* of us. Get what I mean?"

"Cool it," Whiz said wearily. The others looked at him.

Phoebe said, "You smoked it pretty well for a while there, Whiz."

"Yeah," Wu added, still grumpy. "Okay job. For a while at least."

"Yes, we have much to be thankful for," said Barney, smiling and holding his arms wide.

"Sure," Dragon said brightly. "For instance,

none of us was sucked up by a sewage truck."

"A honey wagon," said Jose.

"Nobody was washed out to sea by a ferocious undertow, either," said E6.

"Or eaten by a jaguar," said Phoebe.

"Make it *partially* eaten," suggested Delancey.

Phoebe laughed. "Yes, *much* better."

Others offered a few more examples of disasters that had not stricken the thankful Newts. But the jolly stuff died down eventually, and Whiz found everyone looking at him again across an awkward silence.

"Well," he said, "don't get down. We get more chances to turn it around. Okay?"

E6 pounded his glove. "Yeah," he said earnestly. "Next game, I make only *two* errors."

Everyone knew he wasn't joking. *Well,* thought Whiz, *we all have to hope for something.* And as the Newts straggled back to their dormitories, he wondered what *he* hoped for.

6

W*hiz certainly had not* hoped to lose the next game 16–1 to last year's fourth-place team, the Mudcats. However, that is what happened. He felt miserable. His pitches were soft and straight; they floated up to the plate and *begged* to be powdered. The Mudcats obliged, collecting five home runs, three triples, and six doubles among their hits.

Late that night, Whiz lay awake in the dormitory, trying not to hear around him the wildly varied sounds fifteen boys make when they're sleeping. After a long time, he quietly got out of his bed and dressed quickly in sweats and sneakers. Then he went to the large window letting the early spring air into the room. He pushed it further open with well-practiced movements, careful to apply gradual pressure at a particular point off center. The window went up without a sound.

Whiz hopped out, landed with a *thunk* on the grass outside, and scampered off into the closest copse of trees.

It took him only fifteen minutes to wind his way into town, even using an indirect—and secretive—route of back roads. He walked quietly in the shadows of the buildings along the town square until he reached a dark stairway heading down into an alley. He zipped down the steps, paused at a door, unlocked it, and stepped into the dark printery.

Whiz locked the door behind him, then walked through the dark front office and into the small, low-ceilinged space Mr. Dougal called "the composing room" because that was where the type cabinets stood. Here he turned on a lamp.

Whiz was not entirely certain what he had in mind to do, and he did not stop to think too hard about it. Instead, he took a composing stick, put some slugs in it, pulled out a drawer of twelve-point Garamond, and started rapidly assembling line after line of type. There was no sound but the small clicking of the metal type as he dropped each piece into place.

He felt a strange need to hurry but kept reminding himself to slow down, make sure of his letters, take it light and easy, as if he were just playing around. *But I* am *just playing around, aren't I?* he thought. *What else do I think I'm doing?*

Then he found he had finished setting his lines. He justified them quickly, took the form over to the imposing stone, and locked it into a chase with furniture and quoins. He laid the chase in the proof press, squeezed a dot of ink onto a piece of plate glass, spread the ink with a brayer, and rolled it carefully over the type.

For some reason his heart was beating hard.

He did not reach for one of the newsprint scraps usually used for proofs. Instead, he went quickly into the dark press room, struck a match near the stock shelves, searched for a flat box, and from it took a thick 5" x 8" sheet of white parchment.

Shaking out the match, he walked silently back to the proof press. He drew a deep breath, laid the parchment evenly on the inked form, and rolled the platen over it. He let out the breath as he felt the *ump* of the impression pushing into the paper.

Slowly, his hand shaking slightly with his rapid heartbeat, he rolled the platen back and carefully peeled the piece of parchment away from the type.

Holding his breath, Whiz read the card, then set it aside and began to wash the proof press. When it was clean, he washed and unlocked the form, stored the quoins and furniture, then distributed the type.

He cleaned his hands. Before turning out the light, he picked up the new card and read it again, once, twice. He shook his head. Then he pulled out the pack of Newt cards from the hiding place, inserted the new one into the middle, put them all back, and left.

ACE JONES

BREADHURST NEWTS
PITCHER
BATS: L   THROWS: L
HT: 5'2" WT: 90 LBS.

Ace is a superb fireballer, with
unusual control for a hurler
with his kind of speed. Quiet,
dedicated, and smart, he hits
and fields well, too.

7

Whiz always tried to arrive at the practice field before the other players. He thought it was appropriate for the unofficial captain to do several small things to prepare for play, dropping the bases, cleaning up the baselines, scouring the plate so it was visible. He also brought most of the bats and balls in a large denim sack.

But today, as he approached the field from behind a hillock twenty minutes before practice, he suddenly stopped in his footprints. Before he got over the hilltop, he heard the sound of a ball hitting the backstop in the field at regular intervals. And, if his ear was as good as he thought, hitting it at considerable speed.

He jogged to the top of the hill and stared at the infield. There, on the pitcher's mound, halfway through his windup, was a left-handed boy wearing a Newt cap and shirt over blue jeans. As Whiz watched, the boy snapped through his windup, and with an arm that Whiz saw only as a blur he whipped the ball straight across the plate and *kunch* into the chain-link backstop.

It was the hardest pitch Whiz had ever seen a kid throw with such control.

When Whiz swung his eyes back to the mound, he found that the kid was looking right at him. The kid grinned, waved, and said, "Hey, Whiz," in a casual voice.

Hey, Whiz.

His legs trembled like wind chimes. *How on*

earth did this kid— "What's up—*Ace?*" he heard himself say.

"Not much." The kid shrugged. "Just getting limber, you know."

"Sure," said Whiz. He took a quick look around the entire field. Yes, it was the same old place. He looked back at Ace as the boy walked toward the backstop to collect the half dozen balls that lay behind the plate. Whiz noted that his spikes left prints behind him, and that he cast a shadow. Definitely not Southpaw Dracula.

But *real*, for sure. Called forth from Whiz's imagination and desire, a genuine flesh-and-bones kid, complete with the talents specified.

Whiz knew that he should probably feel like God, or at least like an alchemist or something. Instead, all he could feel like was a printer.

Something caught Whiz's eye on the edge of the field beyond right. Phoebe, Wren, and Delancey were coming.

Whiz hustled down the hill he was standing on. To Ace, once more on the mound with balls, he called, "Hey, I'll catch you up."

"Great."

Whiz ran back and crouched behind the plate.

The first pitch hit his glove and made the leather close over the ball automatically; otherwise he never would have caught it, because he had not even *seen* it. The second pitch, over the black edge on the outside of the plate (a place where Whiz wished he could place *his* pitches), got by him. Then he remembered a trick from playing goalie in ice hockey: If you see the puck come off the shooter's stick, you should be able to stop it. Whiz started concentrating on Ace's left hand throughout the whole windup and found that if he watched the ball all the way to its moment of release, he could position himself to catch it. But whew. These balls came *fast*.

Looking out past Ace, Whiz watched the girls

approaching closer and closer. He saw their eyes on the new pitcher, who did not see them. Whiz waited until the last possible moment, when he saw that Delancey was about to speak; then he stood up.

"Hey, come on, meet our new guy, Ace."

Ace turned and smiled. The girls did not. Whiz went on, before Ace could possibly amaze everyone by reciting their names as he had Whiz's own. "Ace, meet Phoebe, who plays first, Wren, who plays third, and Delancey, second base."

"Sure," said Ace, giving Whiz a quick look, then resuming his grin toward the girls.

"Ace is a day student at Bread," Whiz said. "I found him playing pickup with some older guys in town."

Ace watched with a wrinkle in his forehead as Whiz spoke. He held Whiz in his gaze for an extra second, then looked at the girls and nodded.

A voice from behind said, "Are townies legal?"

Whiz turned to see Barney and Wu standing there. He assumed they had heard his explanation of Ace's sudden presence, so he hastened to introduce them.

Barney smiled, Wu frowned, but they both shook the pitcher's hand. Whiz slyly checked their faces to see if they gave any reaction to touching his flesh—was he cold as the tomb, or metallic as a robot? Apparently not.

"And oh, yeah," Whiz said, turning to Barney, "everything's cool. Townies are okay by league rules. I, like, checked it all out."

"With everybody but us," Wu said, but without any real challenge behind it.

"Wu, why don't you go back there and catch Ace up for a few throws?" Whiz suggested.

Wu gave Ace an unsmiling appraisal, shrugged, then went behind the plate and crouched.

"Air it out," Whiz said to Ace as he took the mound.

"Still getting warm," Ace said.

Whiz watched him throw a dozen pitches. *If he gets much warmer, the ball will start disappearing before it gets to the plate,* he thought. Ace stopped when Wu held up a dark-pink hand of surrender, stood, and walked to the mound. He took Ace's left arm in his hand.

"Special surgery or something?" he said.

Ace laughed and shook his head. "Just got a strong one, I guess. Surprises me as much as it does you."

Wu carefully lowered Ace's arm. "Ray gun," he said. "Our secret weapon."

"Comes complete with cap and shirt and number," said a new voice, and Whiz turned to see E6. The shortstop was staring at Whiz, not at Ace. "Amazing."

"Ain't it though," said Whiz, meeting E6's stare.

"Who wants to bat against him first?" said Dragon, who had drifted up.

"I caught him," said Wu. "I'll hit him."

Whiz held up his hands. "Wait. I thought I'd throw BP as usual—we have a game in two days and we ought to save Ace for that." Most of the players nodded; none seemed too eager to step in against the new kid. Whiz had another reason for letting them take their whacks at his slow balls: He did not want the Newts losing confidence in their hitting, which would certainly happen with Ace busting the ball past them.

With a shimmer Whiz suddenly felt how wonderfully complicated things could grow on a *real* baseball team, with this skill balanced beside that capability, with people who could be counted on for more than three errors or four strikeouts a game. He sighed, and welcomed Ace silently. Maybe, Whiz thought, just maybe he was onto something.

JOSIAH BERG

Breadhurst Newts
Catcher
Bats: R   Throws: R
Ht: 5'5" Wt: 120 lbs.

Jose jumped at the chance to play the hardest position on the diamond and works as hard as anyone in the league. His arm is legendary. A great student of baseball lore, he is always cheerful and ready to play.

On *Saturday morning,* as the team began to show up at the home field of the Bengals, the champions of the league, Whiz watched with anxiety to see if the unexplained trick had really worked—would Ace show up? Whiz did not have long to be nervous. The new pitcher arrived in a foursome, chatting easily with Dragon, Wu, and Barney. Ace greeted the other Newts naturally. They greeted him almost as casually. In the bottom of the first, after the Newts had gone down in order, Ace took the mound for the first time, without a word being said.

Whiz had designated himself benchwarmer for the game. He watched Ace warm up—his first few half-speed throws, just to limber up the arm, were hotter than anything Whiz managed in even his best innings. He shook his head. By the time the first Bengal stepped in to bat, the ball was starting to look extremely small as it darted over the corners of the plate.

It looked that way to the hitter, too. He took two blazing strikes, then swung way early on a high change-up Ace dangled in front of his eyes.

The next batter, after watching one pitch cut the heart of the plate in a blur, tried to bunt the second, merely holding out his bat. But the ball was thrown with such velocity that the impact with the bat, deadened though it was in the hitter's hands, sent it on the fly right back at Ace, who gloved it casually. The third batter touched nothing on his first two swings, then mightily foul-tipped one into Josiah's mitt for another strikeout.

A very tall, very thin girl named Moriah pitched for the Bengals. Her delivery seemed to twist her long body into a coil, so that when she whipped out of it, the ball was slung at the plate with a kind of twisty force that fooled almost everyone in the league. However, it took more than that to fool E6 for long. He led off the second by crushing a drive up the left-field line and chugging into second standing up.

Barney, tall and graceful and strong, looked as if the last thing he would ever do was bunt. So when he dragged one up the first-base line, he caught the Bengals by surprise—Moriah never moved to cover first, and it was only a great twisting tag by the first baseman, who had fielded the ball in her bare hand, that got him out. But his purpose was accomplished: E6 was on third with only one out.

The infield was playing back, conceding the run on a grounder. Phoebe promptly spanked a sharp one, driving the shortstop back to his left behind second. He threw her out, but the run scored, and the Newts had their second lead in as many games. Wren popped out to the catcher to end the inning.

"The damage is done!" Dragon crowed as the Newts took the field.

"Not all of it, I hope," said Whiz.

But as the game went on through the fifth, that was in fact how it looked: The Bengals kept going down in front of Ace, with a single here and there, an error or two, but never did they get a runner past second, and never did they score. Unfortunately, neither did the Newts. Moriah's curving stuff stumped them as badly as Ace's flame burned the Bengals.

Ace took the mound in the bottom of the sixth with three outs to get, for the Newts' first victory by the unlikely score of 1–0.

There is one problem that often crops up in late innings for a pitcher who throws smoke: Hitters who have been watching the ball whiz by them for three at-bats, swinging late and missing, get closer and closer to judging the speed of the ball. Sometimes, they adjust their eye and swing in time to get in some good cuts in their final at-bats.

The Bengals were not champions by accident. Their hitters were patient, opportunistic. The first batter, hitting right-handed, was a little late on one pitch but caught it fat anyway and sent Dragon deep along the line in right. Incredibly, Dragon made a running catch. But the next batter hit the ball just as hard, where no one could catch it—over the left-field fence. As he rounded the bases, he grinned at Ace and yelled, "The harder you throw 'em, the farther they go."

The home run was deflating—but the game

was still tied, and by getting two more outs, the Newts would get a chance to break it in extra innings. It looked good when the next batter smacked a one-hopper to the sure-handed Delancey. It looked awful a moment later, when she bobbled the ball and lost it over her shoulder into shallow right. The runner never stopped, and made it all the way to third by the time Dragon had charged in and lofted a weak off-line throw to Wren.

Moriah came to the plate. Whiz, watching from the bench, recalled that she could whip the bat with the same kind of power she put behind her pitches. He also remembered that she tended to swing wildly. He hoped she would swing so wildly, she wouldn't make even bad contact this time—a fly ball, or even a deep grounder, would score the winning run. Ace had to strike her out. That was all.

She missed the first two pitches by a foot. The

third pitch was low and outside but she yanked it two hundred feet on a line to Wu in left. He caught it, uncorked a fairly good throw, but the runner on third tagged up and scored standing up while Josiah stood waiting for the ball.

Whiz watched Ace pull his cap over his eyes and tromp off the mound with his head down. Whiz walked out to meet him.

"Don't sweat it, man. You were the *best*, the best we've ever had."

When Ace started to look up, Whiz wouldn't have been surprised by almost any expression on his face—anger, disappointment, a rueful smile. But Whiz was not ready for the look on the pitcher's face, and it stopped him flat-footed.

Ace was a complete blank. His eyes looked right through Whiz without a trace of liveliness; his lips looked as if they had been drawn with a pencil; his skin was pale despite the effort of pitching a tough half inning. No muscle twitched, no wrinkle formed.

Ace stayed this way for several seconds. Then, before Whiz's eyes, some color and expression returned to the pitcher's face; his look sharpened; he managed a half smile.

As Josiah and Delancey and Phoebe closed in to offer condolences, Ace finally responded to Whiz, albeit pretty feebly. "Yeah, whatever," he said.

Whiz backed away but watched as Ace stood in the same place, nodding and saying very little as everyone on the team clapped him on the back or said something brief. Ace did not speak. And as soon as the last person left him—Barney, who was trying without success to get a conversation going—he tugged his cap back down over his face and walked off in the direction opposite the way to Breadhurst. Almost all the Newts watched him go. But when Whiz turned to them, thinking of something good to tell them about the loss, he found that one person was paying more attention to him than to Ace.

E6 had him locked in a stare of curiosity. Whiz looked away and started to talk about playing under pressure.

9

The Newts lost the next two games 2–0 and 4–2. Each time, Ace pitched beautifully; each time, a few of the Newts managed singles or doubles; each time, these hits were not enough.

After the games, Ace behaved exactly as he had following the 2–1 loss to the Bengals. And Whiz was no longer alone in noticing the strangeness.

He found Wren at his side as they watched Ace walking away alone after the 4–2 game.

"What's the android-stiff thing about, anyway?" she said.

Whiz nearly leaped straight up. His heart jerked a few times, but he sounded cool enough as he said, "Everybody takes hard defeats differently. I guess he's pretty drained. He kind of gives it all on the mound, don't you think?"

Wren shrugged. "We all play hard. But he's the only one who acts like somebody turned his switch to *off.*" She frowned. "Makes it pretty hard to do the teammate-buddy-warmth thing."

Before Whiz could reply, he saw that E6 had joined them. The shortstop had heard Wren's comment. He cut Whiz off.

"Makes it pretty hard even to do the *human-being* thing." He looked at Whiz, then turned his eyes in the direction Ace had taken. "I almost wonder if he's gone back to some giant test tube, where he'll get his fluids changed before the next game."

Whiz shivered but tried to make it look as if he were shaking with a laugh. "What mad scientist would take the trouble to manufacture a pitcher for the Breadhurst Newts?"

"A *really* mad one," said Wren.

"Not so mad he can't give his creature a wicked fastball," said E6. He nodded toward the distance that contained Ace somewhere. "I mean, think about it—can you see Frankenstein with pinpoint control? The Relic with a slider?"

"He's just a moody kid," said Whiz, "who can play the game."

"Which game?" said E6, looking innocent. Then he quickly added, "Oh, you mean *baseball.* Oh, right, yes."

Wren gave him a weird look, but E6 just smiled, nodded at them both, and left.

"Does he know something we don't?" Wren asked, with a sarcasm that relieved Whiz.

"Shortstops are strange," he said with a laugh. "Like goalies in hockey."

Wren shrugged again and turned to go. "Well,

at least we know E is *human.* You can't argue with the evidence for *that.*"

"What evidence?" said Whiz carefully.

"He makes lots of errors," Wren said over her shoulder. "Whereas Ace is a little *perfect,* maybe." Then she was gone.

"Perfect," Whiz said to himself. He shook his head. "Just *perfect.*"

DIANA FULLER

B<small>READHURST</small> N<small>EWTS</small>
O<small>UTFIELD</small>
B<small>ATS</small>: B<small>OTH</small> T<small>HROWS</small>: R
H<small>T</small>: 5'5" W<small>T</small>: 120 <small>LBS</small>.

Diana has muscle (she was a
champion gymnast at 8), a
great eye, and killer timing—
all of which make her one of
the best pure hitters in the
league. She bats around .450,
but her power is awesome: She
averages two extra-base hits
and three RBI per game.
Dedicated, confident—and a
WINNER.

10

In the pool of light from the small lamp, with the typecases and dark presses looming around him like mystery itself, Whiz read the parchment card three times. Then he put it among the others in their hiding place, turned out the light, and left silently.

11

Whiz made sure he was the first Newt to arrive for practice the next day. He came an hour early, with eight new balls—enough so that someone (say, a power hitter) could lose a few over the distant hills. To kill the time while he waited, he took four balls and pitched them over the plate. But it felt weird being on the mound. He realized that the place no longer belonged to him. Already it was Ace's spot.

Whiz retrieved the balls, then waited by the bench.

He wasn't surprised, a half hour later, when the figure of Ace came suddenly over the hill on the third-base side. And he tried hard not to be surprised when another figure walked over the crest a few steps behind the pitcher.

A tall kid. Wearing a Newt cap and T-shirt, with the sleeves cut off. Girl. Long arms; it looked as if unbreakable cables and cords ran beneath the cedar-colored skin. Same with the legs—calf muscles like tennis balls. As Whiz looked up, a smile popped out on the face—brilliant eyes, wide mouth, great cheekbones. She was beautiful. And she was carrying a large bat as if it were a wooden spoon.

"Hey, Whiz," she said.

"Hi—*Diana*," he said with a quiver. "Hey, Ace."

"'S up, Whizzer."

So there they were. Whiz just stared for a few seconds, as Ace took the mound and Diana moved toward the plate. Then, with a dry mouth, Whiz went further.

"Going to launch some of your moon shots, or are you saving your power for Saturday?"

Diana laughed. "Save power?" she said. "No need. See, I have an endless supply." She gave Whiz an amused look.

He tried not to squirm. Instead, he picked up his glove and started to trot out to center field. "I'll chase," he said. "Blast away."

He was still trotting, with his back to the plate, when she hit the first one. He heard the *whock* of the bat and barely had time to look up and see the ball as it flew over him at some huge height, with some huge force. He glanced back to see them both watching him. He turned back and ran after the ball. And ran. He finally came upon it halfway down the hill bordering dead center.

He bounced a long throw back to Ace. "Nice poke," he yelled.

Diana nodded as she took her stance. Ace wound up and threw, hard. Even from deep center, Whiz could see the fierce flash in Diana's eyes as she watched the ball coming. Then he saw some sort of circular motion, incredibly fast, and heard another *whock*. This time the ball arched long and high to the deepest part of left field.

"Who is *that?*"

Whiz turned. Delancey, Dragon, and E6 had come over the hilltop. They stared at the ball until it rolled over the crest in left, then switched their eyes to the distant hitter.

"I repeat, in an inquiring tone," said Dragon, "who is *that?*"

Whiz gave each of them a glance. "It's—she— her name is Diana. She was a gymnast, but—but she grew too tall to keep at it. So she took up baseball. And she found out she was, like, a natural power hitter."

"And strangely enough, she never joined a

team," said E6, "nor was she discovered by any other kids, until *you* happened to see her in some lonely sandlot, hitting three-hundred-foot line drives in total obscurity."

Whiz returned the shortstop's challenging stare. "Actually, I didn't 'discover' her. She's a friend of Ace's. He told her about the team, and she asked for a tryout."

Behind them came the sound of bat crushing ball. Whiz ducked, then turned to see a sharp liner dipping to the ground in right, taking a first bounce that had more force than most of the other Newts' hits on the *fly*.

"I vote she stays," said Dragon. "In fact, she can have right field. I'll be a full-time heckler from the bench."

Whiz saw Barney and Wu come over the crest behind the backstop. They stopped and watched Diana crack another one. They looked at each other, then watched her. Phoebe, Wren, and

Josiah came up in right. Phoebe was holding a ball in her outstretched hand, as if displaying a dinosaur skull—*Look what I found out here; can you imagine?*

Whiz jogged in and introduced Diana to the others. They all greeted her with the same kind of careful enthusiasm they had used to welcome Ace. But this time it appeared to Whiz that each of them faced a quick decision: whether to feel *weirder* about another mystery player, or to accept it and feel accustomed.

It seemed as if they all chose *accustomed.*

Practice started. Whiz talked with Ace, and they decided it might be best for Whiz to pitch batting practice again—not to save Ace's arm, Whiz thought, but to make sure the Newts got pitches they could hit. Ace wandered around in short center, grabbing liners that would have been singles if he hadn't been there, politely calling out, "Nice rope!" or "Good bingle!" to make up for robbing the batter. Diana was out in right, talking to Dragon, both of them laughing occasionally. Dragon was not wearing his glove—Diana was. Every time a ball was hit her way, Whiz watched her snap into concentration and zero in for the catch.

He called her in to hit after Josiah had taken his cuts. A slight stillness hovered over the field as she ran in, picked out her bat, and stood up, batting left-handed, to face Whiz's fat ones.

From behind him, Whiz heard E6's voice: "Why am I not surprised she switches?"

To which Wren replied, "Another perfect one."

Whiz pitched.

Diana watched the first pitch all the way into Josiah's mitt, getting an idea of the ball's pace— a pace that, Whiz imagined, she must find incredible. She had already shown she could clobber Ace's swifties; what would she do to Whiz's sweet offerings?

She would *launch* them, that's what. Starting with the second pitch, all the way through the tenth, Diana, eyes flashing, spun through her circular-saw swing and drove the ball high and hard to all fields. Four of them sailed over the hill-tops on the fly—uncontested home runs in the field's ground rules. The others kept the out-fielders running, lunging, running some more.

After her last poke, Diana gave Whiz a big grin, then put her bat down with the others and trotted out to right. There was an odd moment of silence, then Whiz heard handclaps. He turned and saw Wren looking off toward Diana and applauding. E6 joined her. So, surprisingly, did Wu. Soon everyone was clapping. Diana, standing out in right by this time, looked straight ahead toward the infield. Then, in a quick motion, she raised her cap and put it back on her head.

The clapping stopped. "Um, Barney," Whiz called out with a croak. Barney jogged in to hit.

After practice, Dragon was the first person to reach Whiz. "Let me remind you of what I said earlier, Swami. I am resigning from right field so that I may devote myself full-time to the bench position of M and A Coach."

Whiz wrinkled his forehead. "M and A?"

"Morale and Abuse," Dragon said, eyes foxy behind his glasses. "Someone has to do the dirty work, and I was born for this purpose." He handed his glove to Whiz, bowed, and left.

Whiz looked out toward right. Wu, Barney, and Phoebe were talking with Diana. Ace was walking out to join them. Wu was going through ghost swings and asking Diana something, evidently about wrists.

E6 appeared. He was watching the group in right too. "Gymnastics, hm?" he said. "To think she might have wasted her life turning flips. I'd say we're saving her, really. Imagine using that eye only to read textbooks."

Whiz looked at his friend, then around the field. "Yeah, well. She can certainly hit. We should be grateful Ace recruited her."

"Ace? Recruited her? Really?" said E6, raising his eyebrows at Whiz.

"Yes, really," Whiz said, on the verge of anger. "What's your problem with—"

"With them," E6 finished. "That's right, isn't it? They are *them*. They aren't *us*. That's how it feels to everyone, before we remember to be chummy with our new teammates. I can't help wondering why things feel so weird. I can't help wondering where these dream-come-true players *were*."

"Things feel weird because all of us from last year, all of us from school, have had to open the circle for a couple of more talented strangers. It's bound to take a while before everybody feels comfortable. I'd say we're doing pretty well."

E6 nodded as if Whiz had said something new and vaguely interesting. Then he said, "And as to where they were? Where they *came from*? Why they appeared so suddenly, as if in answer to our hottest wish? Maybe I'm too curious, but—"

"You *are* too curious," Whiz said decisively. "What do you want, a pedigree listing their, like, lineage? Photos of the grandparents? Come on, E. You're not so inquisitive about Delancey or Wu or Jose, are you?"

"I've been friends with everyone on this team for four years," E6 said. "You don't have to be inquisitive with good friends—you just get to know stuff. It rubs off during all the time you spend together."

"So spend some time with Ace and Diana and give stuff a chance to rub off. What's your big rush?" said Whiz. "We have a great new pitcher and now a great new hitter. Why worry?"

E6 was silent for a moment, looking at Whiz. Then he said, "Okay, Whizzer. Let's see if our new thoroughbreds can make good buddies. With *us,*

I mean." He pointed. Ace and Diana were walking down the hill, alone together. "They seem to be fairly comfortable with each other."

Whiz shook his head and started to walk back toward the rest of the team. "Who cares? They seem to be comfortable throwing aspirins and swatting taters. That's enough for me."

"Is it?" E6 called from behind him. "Is it really enough?"

PHOEBE JAMES

Breadhurst Newts
First Base
Bats: L Throws: L
Ht: 5'2" Wt: 90 lbs.

The rock of the infield,
Phoebe handles all those
throws from all those fielders
the same way: She catches
them, with sure hands. She is
one of the best clutch hitters
on the Newts, the one her
teammates like to see at the
plate in a key situation. Her
intelligence and dedication
inspire everyone on the field.

12

Whiz *couldn't wait* for the next game. Neither, apparently, could the other Newts—the last to arrive was Josiah, and even he was thirty minutes early. Ace and Diana came together in the middle of the arrivals.

This was the halfway point in the season—from now on, the teams repeated their earlier schedule, with the home fields reversed. Today's opponent was the Hawks once again. In their first game, Whiz had held the Hawk hitters in check pretty well for a few innings. It stood to reason that if *he* had been even a *little* effective against them, then Ace, whom they had never seen, would blow them clean away.

In the top of the first, that's exactly what happened. Whiz, playing second because Delancey had a cold, got a great view of the amazed looks on the faces of the Hawk hitters as all three struck out, looking bad.

In the bottom of the inning, E6 yanked a double down the third-base line with two out. Diana, batting clean-up, stepped to the plate. Josiah hollered, *"Tater! Round-tripper! Go deep!"* But everyone else on the bench watched with a tense anticipation.

For this game, the Hawks started the fat, flushed redhead who had closed out the first game with the Newts. He had thrown hard and wild that day, intimidating the hitters; he was throwing even harder and wilder today. Dragon had found out his name was Bart and, for the first three Newt at-bats, had been calling him "Beet." Now, Dragon modified Josiah's plea for a tater and called out, *"Tuber! Tuber!"*

The first pitch came in fast and inside. Without even straightening up to get farther out of its way, Diana watched it pass two inches from her knees and disappear into the catcher's mitt. The next pitch sailed past the catcher and umpire, hitting the backstop six feet up. E6 trotted to third.

The third pitch failed to meet either the catcher's mitt or the backstop. Instead, the ball reached the section of fence in deep right center on the fly, because that is where Diana's huge bat, swung in a blur, airmailed it. E6 walked to the plate, watching the outfielders chase the ball, then whooped as he stomped on the plate. Diana cruised into second standing up. The rest of the Newts sprang off the bench with hoots and hollers, fists shooting up, hands waving. Diana looked straight ahead with a small smile.

Phoebe hit the fat kid's first pitch hard on the ground between the shortstop and third baseman. The shortstop made a grand dive at the ball, but it ticked off the end of his glove and rolled into left field. Diana, running on contact with two down, scored easily. Josiah popped to shallow right, stranding Phoebe on second. But the Newts were happy—they had given Ace a couple of runs to work with.

He seemed to appreciate it. The Hawks managed a walk in the second, a bloop double to right in the third, and a blind-swing home run by the catcher in the fifth. That was it. Meanwhile, the Newts, inspired by another blast from Diana— this one a three-run homer in the third—mauled Beet one after another, piling up the gaudy total of nine runs. Phoebe added two more singles to her first hit; Wu tripled and doubled, driven in both times by E6; Whiz poked two doubles and scored both times on sharp singles from Josiah. Even Dragon, pinch-hitting for Whiz in the fifth, reached on a seeing-eye bouncer that eluded the right side of the Hawk infield, dribbling into shallow right.

When it was over, for a moment the old Newts were unable to decide whether they should celebrate their first victory in two seasons by going nuts, or by playing it cool. They took their cue from the heroes of the game, the two new Newts. They watched Diana and Ace, calmly acting as if winning were the *expected* thing, smiling and offering low-key congratulations all around. The players who thought that a miracle had struck the team and were inclined to bounce and yell about it swallowed their excitement and tried to take it easy.

Whiz walked back to the Breadhurst campus with E6. "Good game, E," he said as they left the field.

E6 looked sideways at him. "Yeah," he said, "the bats woke up. Diana's magic, isn't she?"

Whiz couldn't stop a frown. "What do you—"

"I mean, whatever mysterious gift she has, she can spread it around like a virus."

Whiz winced. "How about 'like a tune you can't forget' or—"

"Whatever," said E6. He walked a few steps before adding, "All I can say is, she and Ace are pretty powerful. And it feels strange to be pulled into it."

"It's called 'charisma' or 'spirit' or 'magnetism,'" said Whiz. "The great players have it, and inspire it in their teammates. And it's perfectly *natural,* E."

"I wouldn't call Ace and Diana charismatic, unless you get a thrill from watching dry ice as it doesn't melt," said E6. "And dry ice ain't natural, either."

Whiz gave a heavy sigh. "We won. Congratulations, buddy. Okay?"

E6 looked at him and shrugged. "Sure. Okay. Buddy."

They walked the rest of the way without speaking.

LOUIE WU

BREADHURST NEWTS
LEFT FIELD
BATS: BOTH   THROWS: L
HT: 5'3" WT: 110 LBS.

Wu is a terror at the plate—he
led the team in homers and
doubles last season. In the
field he gets to everything and
throws with great power.
Aggressive, gritty, hard-nosed,
Wu takes no prisoners. His
attitude makes him a mean
leader.

13

*T*he *next two games* made the Newts' cool attitude seem reasonable. They beat the Mudcats and the Bengals with style, 7–2 and 5–1. Ace was superb both times; all the runs against him were unearned, thanks to a total of eleven Newt errors. Diana continued to murder the ball—in fact, she drove in all five runs against the Bengals, with four hits.

These heroics made Whiz a little uneasy, despite the joy of winning the games. He noticed that the old Newts were quickly falling back into their old ways; the great performance of Ace and Diana became commonplace, and thus less of an awesome, inspiring thing. Obviously, the two new players were carrying the rest of them. The old Newts, Whiz knew, carried nothing but a fate for ugly errors, woeful pop-ups, and pitiful strikeouts.

Whiz was reminded that the limits of one's skill were not vaulted simply because the team managed to win a few games: Ace, tired, asked him to pitch the game after the Bengals win, and Whiz proceeded to get hammered for six runs in two innings. Ace came on and shut the Sharks down for the last four; Diana doubled in three runs with two out in the bottom of the sixth, to go with her solo home runs in the third and fifth. The Newts ended up winning 7–6. That was too close for Whiz, with too much focus on one pitcher and one hitter.

And four errors by E6 were too many; so were

three by Wu, and five passed balls that blew by Josiah. Everyone misplayed at least one chance in the Sharks game. *The errors are the biggest threat,* Whiz thought; *the errors will kill us.*

Everyone knew it. Josiah summed it up. "The leather is a little leaky," he said.

Dragon laughed. "A little? If 'the leather' were a boat, it would be growing barnacles at the bottom of the Atlantic."

Delancey, who fielded well, said, "Nobody's *interested* in getting better at catching and throwing. It's all *hitting* and *pitching*. Always has been, always will be. The stars are the hitters and pitchers." She laughed with a bitter tinge. "This team could use some *fielders*."

"Hey, I'm ready," said Wu.

"And I," said E6, looking at Whiz, "am even *expectant*."

Whiz just tapped his fist into his glove.

MAX AND MARTY ROJAS

BREADHURST NEWTS
THIRD BASE, SHORTSTOP
BAT: R THROW: R
HT: 5'5" WT: 125 LBS.

Just try to poke the ball past this Keystone Combo. Twins by birth, they are identical in fielding genius, too.

As *Whiz was leaving*—very early—for the last practice before the next game, he was nabbed by E6, who needed help rethreading the thong in the heel of his glove. Whiz could hardly refuse. When they finished, there was just time to get to practice twenty minutes early.

When they came over the hill with the field in front of them, E6 immediately said, "*Two* of them? Who are they?"

Ace and Diana were talking on the pitcher's mound. With them, wearing Newt caps far back on their thick black hair, were two dark-skinned, large-eyed boys who looked precisely alike. They were chewing gum with their mouths open, spitting now and then, nodding at Ace as he spoke—they were right at home.

"They are Max and Marty Rojas," Whiz said. "Twins." As if they had heard him, the two new faces turned his way. He waved. The four intense eyes seemed to study him quickly. Then the Rojas boys turned back to their talk with Ace and Diana.

"Sweet dudes, I see," said E6. "They'll fit right in. Let me guess—they're friends of Ace's; he found them playing some dynamite stickball in the mean streets."

Whiz reddened slightly. "Actually, they are Diana's friends. From church or something, I think."

"Ah," said E6, nodding. "She stole them from the choir, no doubt. And what talents do the

Rojas boys possess, I wonder?"

"Well," said Whiz, "I hear they are really superb fielders."

"Superb fielders," said E6 appreciatively. "Now *that's* a good idea."

Whiz looked at him and tried to frown angrily. "They're not 'ideas,' E—they are *players.*"

"Interesting that you said 'players' instead of 'people.'" Before Whiz could reply, E6 went on. "Now, my next question has to do with the place on the field where these fabulous twins work their glove magic. Are they by any chance *infielders?*"

"I hear—I think, yes, that's where they usually play—"

"Sort of a natural 'Keystone Combo,' aren't they? But that would mean Delancey would have to move, and she's already so good at second. Then—let me guess—do these guys play shortstop and third base?"

Whiz reddened again. By this time other players were arriving. Some steered clear of the mound and just stared; some walked over and introduced themselves to Max and Marty. Whiz sighed and said, "Yes, E. That's where they play. Short and third. We'll give them a tryout, nothing is definite—"

"Oh, of course not," said E6. "But something tells me they will perform *perfectly*. Somehow I bet they will indeed win our jobs, if not our hearts. And for the new, improved version of the Breadhurst Newts—or maybe we should drop the school affiliation, what with so many stars from town—for the new improved Newts, they will be just what the doctor ordered."

By this time Whiz and E6 were walking across the infield toward the mound. They said hello to Ace and Diana, who gave them nods and brief smiles, and then introduced themselves to the twins. Who gave them nods, but no smiles.

"Hey, sorry if we, like, intruded on some-thing," said E6 in a goody-goody tone.

"No problem," said Ace.

"We'll be ready in a minute, okay?" said Diana.

"Okay," said E6, and turned on his heel. He and Whiz walked to the bench.

Whiz explained Max and Marty to the old Newts. They just looked at him with a kind of resignation.

Both groups broke up and took the field. Whiz took the mound. E6 asked to bat first. Marty stepped into the shortstop position like a male dog that has marked his spot. Max crouched beside Wren in super-ready-on-my-toes-got-it-covered mode. Wren stared at him for a minute. Then she looked over at Whiz and rolled her eyes. He smiled. She walked across the baseline and sat on the grass.

Whiz turned to the plate. E6 was in his

stance. Whiz could see that his friend was tightly wound, ferociously concentrated. *This guy can hit,* Whiz thought. *He can do what he wants with my pitches.*

As if to confirm Whiz's thought, E6 smashed his first pitch right at Marty. It was a nasty, spinning two-hopper that would handcuff most infielders. But Marty made room by springing back, away from the ball, and taking it on his backhand, facing the outfield. He completed his turn, stopped, and whipped a very hot sidearm throw to Phoebe, who said "Ow!" when she caught it.

E6 pulled the next pitch on a line over third. It looked as if Max leaped simultaneously with the sound of the hit; certainly he was stretched high very quickly. At the top of his long form, his glove jerked toward the outfield. He landed, opened the glove to show the ball for a half second, then tossed it to his brother for a trip around the infield.

E6 manged to pepper the twins with nine of his ten pitches. He sent them low to snag grass-cutting liners; he backed them up and made them catch flies over their shoulders; he made them charge and field the ball one-handed; he froze them with pokes right in their eyes. They handled it all with an insufferable air of casualness. When his cuts were through, E6 placed his bat carefully with the others, walked to the bench, and sat, back straight, hands in his lap.

"Get it all, Whizzer," he said.

Whiz felt like mud.

For the rest of the practice, the Rojas boys continued to show their stuff whenever any-thing was hit anywhere close to them. When practice was over, they showed the same blank-ness the old Newts had come to expect from Ace and Diana, but with an extra twist of cockiness, almost arrogance. Whiz was tense about their bold attitude; he was relieved when the four new players left together.

In the back of his mind, he knew that was not the way he ought to feel about teammates. But, man, they were *good*!

EDDIE MARCHANT

BREADHURST NEWTS
SHORTSTOP
BATS: L THROWS: R
HT: 5'3" WT: 115 LBS.

"E6" is simply the best hitter
on the Newts and one of
the league leaders. He batted
nearly .500 last season, leading
the team in hits, runs scored,
total bases, and runs batted in.
One of the team's founders, he
has a brilliant overview of the
team and its strengths that
makes him practically a
manager.

Now the Newts became a terror. They won their next two games 3–0 and 4–1, with E6 replacing Phoebe at first for the second game and getting four hits. Always before, he had claimed he could hit well only when he was playing short in the field—but one game on the bench seemed to broaden his attitude. Whiz sat more than anyone, but tried to get everyone playing time, hoping to dampen any potential resentment of all the new starters. He worked Wren into right for half of each game, and put Phoebe behind the plate for the second. She put the equipment on right, caught at least as well as Josiah, and collected two singles.

Whiz himself played left field for two innings in the second victory, after Wu was ejected for arguing a called third strike. He batted once, and flied out.

The Newts now had decent, sometimes spectacular defense. They had decent, sometimes spectacular hitting. They had a spectacular pitcher who needed very little relief from a slightly less-than-decent bull pen of one. When Whiz thought about it, he had to conclude—they had pretty much everything, did they not?

Did they? Whiz could believe that all was sunshine only if he ignored the fact that the team was not having fun. The sagging of spirit was obvious— the old Newts now acted like gate-crashing guests at a party thrown by Ace, Diana, Max, and Marty. More and more the Breadhurst contingent ceded something vital—something like *control*—to the mysterious townies. In a way, this was inevitable. After all, the old Newts depended on the new kids to do the heavy hitting, pitching, and fielding.

It was as if they had all been holding a baseball together, and had let it slip out of their hands. The new kids had caught it and put it into play immediately.

Even so, there were only four new Newts, and nine players had to take the field for a game. Whiz kept hoping the contrast between the two groups would decrease, that the skills of Ace, Diana, and the Rojas hotshots would rub off on his friends. But he watched tensely as, instead, the gap grew wider.

The game against the Snakes should have been an easy win for what E6 called the "new, improved Newts." The Snakes had barely finished above the Newts in the standings last season; they had won only two games, behind the pitching of their only great player, a pitcher named Juanita. Juanita did not throw very hard, but she made up for her lack of speed with perfect control and a shrewd sense of how to keep hitters off-balance by mixing the pace and location of her pitches. But even on their smoothly groomed home field, the Snakes booted every third ball, and few could swing the bat well. Whiz knew Ace would mow them down like a Weedwacker attacking tall, dry grass.

Ace did so, with the help of some brilliant stabs by Max, Marty, and Barney. And though most of the Newts were mystified by Juanita, E6 poked a single in the third and Diana followed with a triple. She died on third as Wu fanned on three off-speed pitches. But in the top of the fifth, she added a solo homer.

Ace struck out the side in the bottom of the fifth. The two-run lead was not much, but Whiz hoped it would be enough, even as he recalled the many small leads the Newts had blown in the last inning. Juanita did nothing to settle his hopping stomach, as she matched Ace by getting Josiah, Max, and Marty on strikes.

Ace blew three darts past the wimpy swings of the first batter in the bottom of the sixth. But the third pitch got away from Josiah, and he could not get his mask off cleanly in time to find it, allowing the struck-out batter to reach first. The next hitter topped a weak grounder up the first-base line. E6 charged it, with Ace covering the bag behind him. E6 bobbled the ball, rushed into his throw, and corked it over Ace's head into right. The runners wound up at second and third.

Ace bore down. The next two batters did not touch the ball; Whiz doubted they even saw it. Two down. One out to go. Two-run lead, two runners in scoring position. On the bench, Whiz had a sudden queer feeling as Juanita stepped in to bat. She was a poor hitter; why was he so uneasy?

Ace quickly put two strikes past her. His third pitch was a change-up he obviously meant to waste outside and high. But Juanita lunged at it nervously, and her wild cut made contact. Bad contact—she undercut the ball and sent a high, shallow fly to left. Wu, eyes high, waved Marty off and smacked his glove twice as he moved in five careful steps to take the last out.

Judging fly balls cannot be taught; it is an inner talent, an extra sense. Today, Wu had made four solid catches in left. But the fifth chance was one too many. As Juanita's spinny pop-up came down, Wu suddenly backpedaled two frantic steps and stuck his glove straight up behind him. The ball came down, glanced off, and shot away at a sharp angle to the left, bouncing toward the hilltop.

Wu caught his heel, and fell.

Barney, backing him up, was surprised by the angle of the ball's carom. Pivoting, he decided to try to cut off the bounce and intercept the ball short of the hilltop, instead of chasing it. But he was a half second too late. Everyone watched the ball scuttle past him as he dove, fully stretched. The ball came to a stop on the farthest edge of left field.

All three runners scored before a Newt even touched the ball. Marty ran out and made a valiant heave on three bounces to Josiah, but Juanita had already stomped the plate with the winning run, her fists high as she howled.

Whiz watched Ace as all this unfolded. The pitcher showed no reaction as he followed the ball with his eyes. After Marty's futile throw, Ace, standing still, gave long looks first to Max, then to Diana, who was walking in toward the mound from right. Max was there by the time she arrived, and Marty a moment later; in a tight circle, they spoke briefly and coolly. Then Ace turned, his eyes seeking someone. Whiz wondered who it was, until Ace located *him*, and locked him in a serious look that seemed to convey everything from challenge to disdain.

Then the four players walked off the mound together. They left the field without speaking to anyone.

"Snots," said Wren, standing behind Whiz.

"Extremely unsportsmanlike, no?" added Phoebe.

"You mean *real bush*," said Josiah.

"They played well," Whiz heard himself say. "We let them down."

Wren and Phoebe looked at him as if he had just spit on their shoes. A bitter laugh broke in from the right.

"Let them *down?*" said E6. "We let them on the *team*. You remember—*our* team. They can play, but they have tin for *heart*. If you'll pardon me for mentioning such a thing."

"Cool it," Delancey said wearily. She had her hand on Wu's shoulder; he was sitting in a slump, his head hanging between his knees, cap pulled low. "We have to admit that without them, we wouldn't even have been close enough to let it get away."

"Let *what* get away, exactly?" said E6.

"The game, of course," said Delancey. "Stop acting like Owl in *Winnie-the-Pooh*, E."

E6 ignored her last comment, but seized on her first. "Ah," he said, more owlishly than ever. "Ah, yes. Letting *the game* get away." He grinned at Delancey. "You said it, Lance. You said it all."

"Then you can stop talking," said Delancey.

"And we can all start *playing* again, okay?" said Whiz. He sounded like a priest trying to join a poker game. He got nothing but looks.

Whiz watched his worst fears come true on the field. The Newts won a game 2–0 as Ace threw a cold two-hitter and Diana drove in both runs. Each of the old Newts except Barney committed at least one error. Then came two bad losses, 3–1 and 2–1. In both games, the old curse held: Ace was nearly perfect, Diana did all the hitting, and only the Rojas twins could handle the ball.

The second loss was especially humiliating. Ace pitched a complete game no-hitter, making a solo homer by Diana stand up until the fifth, when E6, Wu, Delancey, and Josiah made errors on consecutive batters and base runners, allowing two unearned runs. The same players failed to hit in the Newt half of the inning, and that was the ball game.

During these three games—even the victory—the separate solidarity of what E6 had begun to call "The Gang of Four" gave off an increasingly exclusive chill. Ace continued to fix Whiz with deep looks, but otherwise there was virtually no communication between the old Newts and the new. Barney, Wu, Delancey, Dragon, Phoebe, Wren, Josiah, E6, and Whiz were left to stew over all their own awkward whiffs in key at-bats, sloppy muffs with men on base, bad throws, and worse decisions, all by themselves. Once, during a bad collective silence after the four had left, Wu said, "I wish they'd just *tell* us we suck." Almost everyone nodded.

Whiz did his best to hold things together as the team approached the final game of the season. "We'll pull it tight for the last one," he told the Breadhurst group. "A win puts us at .500 for the season. Do you realize that? At the start of the season, we would have done *anything* to go halves. Hey, victory will make us all friends again." He smiled around at everyone. "We'll end this show feeling *great!*"

After a moment of silence, Delancey said, "*You* sound like Christopher Robin."

"On a sunny day," added Dragon. "With a mouth full of honey."

Whiz did not reply. He had only one thought: *I'll make sure we get that win.*

By now, the routine of staying awake until late night and sneaking away from school to town was a snap for Whiz. He had become so sure of himself as a cat in the dark that he never even looked behind him to see if anyone had noticed him passing, or—impossible!—to see if anyone followed him. Two nights before the Newts' final game, he cruised into the printery as usual, secure with the sense that he was about to fix everything, for everyone, all by himself.

Thus he was stunned, as he inked the proof

press to print on a piece of parchment the first of three forms he had set, to hear a footfall in the outer office, and to see E6 step into the composing room.

"Ah," said the voice of E6, "the master craftsman at work."

Whiz whirled around. His friend just stood and smiled, managing to look all-knowing despite his outfit of jeans, an inside-out sweatshirt, and untied, unmatched sneakers with no socks. "Sorry," E6 said, pointing to his clothes as Whiz stared. "I had to get dressed in kind of a hurry."

Whiz stammered. "I—how—"

"Pretty easy, really," said E6. "This is actually the third time I've followed you while you were playing Zorro. I just haven't entered the sanctum before." He glanced around, then looked for a long moment at the three forms of type. Raising his eyes to Whiz, he said, "*Amigo*—I have no idea what you are doing. Do *you?*"

Whiz, holding the inky brayer, looked at the proof press and shot a glance at the place where he kept the team cards. "Well," he said, looking back to E6, "yeah. I mean, I know what I *do*, but—" He stopped.

"But you don't know what it *does*." E6 laughed. "This is pretty weird. But you know what? Now you're going to do something you understand."

"What's that?" said Whiz.

"You're going to *stop*."

Whiz shook his head. "No way. It's just one more game, and if—"

E6 kept speaking. "And not only are you going to stop. You're also going to *undo* whatever it is that's made them *happen*."

"No way, E. Just let me go ahead one more time."

"Show me," said E6.

Whiz frowned at him for a moment. Then he shook his head, shrugged, and put down the brayer. He walked to his hiding place and took out the Newt cards.

"Take a look, then," he said, handing them to E6.

E6 took his time, reading each card. When he came to the first card of a new player—Diana— he raised his eyebrows and looked at Whiz. Whiz shrugged and shook his head again. E6 resumed his reading and went all the way through the rest of the cards. He pulled out the cards for Diana, Ace, and Max and Marty, and put them to one side.

When he had finished, he tapped both groups into neat stacks. He sighed. "They're beautiful, Whizzer. Man, the team would be honored. You've put a lot of thought into these, about each of us."

Whiz nodded. "But—?"

E6 put a finger on the small stack. "But *these* have to go." He paused. "Wherever they *can* go."

Whiz coughed out an incredulous laugh. "*What?* You've got to be kidding! I mean, okay, maybe I'll consider not doing the new ones, but these guys—we *need* these guys!"

E6 shook his head. "We need ourselves."

"Don't talk that trash, man. You've got to— Okay, tell me: Where would we be without the four of them?"

"Well," said E6 with a smile, "for *one* thing, we'd be on the *field*."

"Losing games!"

"Having a decent time!"

"Stinking!"

"Playing!"

"You're just honked because Marty took your spot."

"No," said E6. "I'm just honked because some gotta-win weirdo took *your* spot."

Whiz slumped a little. He looked around the room, until the form on the proof press drew his eye.

"Forget it," said E6.

"But listen, E, just let me do—"

"It's over, Whizzer."

Whiz pointed to the form. "But this guy could—"

"It's not a *guy*, you dope!" E6 yelled. "It's a bunch of little pieces of metal."

Whiz said quietly, "But when I print it—"

"It's still an *it*," said E6. "Not a person. Any more than these are. I'll tell you what—Ace wasn't the one who threw smoke. It's *you*. That's all these are—*smoke*." He held up the stack of four cards with both hands, as if he were going to rip them down the middle.

"Don't!"

"We have to drop this wacko stuff and get back—"

"I don't mean that," said Whiz. "I mean, if you tear up the cards—well, it's kind of violent, and I don't know what would happen, you know, to . . ." He trailed off.

E6 turned a little pale. He looked at his hands and lowered them. "Oh. Yeah. Yuck." He frowned. "Am I right in thinking not even *you* know where they came from—or where they, like *are*?"

"Yeah," said Whiz. He looked at E6. Neither spoke for a moment. Then in a small voice Whiz said, "Okay. I'll—we can—it will kind of be a relief, to tell you the truth."

E6 grinned and, in a sweetsy voice, said, "See? Losing 14–2 can be *fun!*"

Whiz smiled. Then he gestured at the cards E6 was holding. "But how do we get rid of them?"

"*I* have no idea," said E6. "I didn't print them in the first place."

Whiz looked at him. "Right," he said, after a moment. "It's about *printing* them." He slid off the stool, grabbed a composing stick, and pulled out a drawer of thirty-six-point type. Quickly he set three lines, made a form on the stone, and put it on the proof press in place of the form that had been there. He looked on a shelf that held curled tubes of ink with various amounts remaining inside, and poked through them.

"What?" said E6.

"Red," said Whiz. He found a tube and squeezed a fat dot of red ink onto another wedge of plate glass. With a clean brayer he rolled it out, then inked the form.

He held out his hand for the cards E6 was holding. E6 did not give them up. "First you have to—"

"First you have to trust me. Give me the cards."

E6 handed them over.

Whiz placed the first card—Ace's—diagonally over the form, and rolled the platen. When he lifted the parchment from the form and held it up, he smiled and said, "That should do it."

"Let me see. What did you do?"

Whiz handed him the card. "Watch it—the ink is wet."

E6 read the red words aloud: *"Traded to Texas for players to be named later."* He laughed. "Ninth-round draft choices and washed-up DH's."

"Exactly," said Whiz. "To be named *much* later."

E6 read the card again as Whiz rolled the other three through the press. When they were printed, E6 asked, "Why Texas?"

Whiz shrugged. "It's far away, it's huge, and they all can get lost there."

"I don't see Diana happy with sweat running into those amazing eyes while she tries to focus on a bender from some beef-fed dude from Dallas."

Whiz shrugged. "Either you get the curve, or the curve gets you."

They cleaned up while the ink dried on the cards. When they were wiping their hands, E6 said, "What should we do with those?"

Whiz thought about it. "I'll save them in a separate envelope."

Then E6 pointed to the other pile. "And those?"

Whiz blushed slightly. "Those I kind of keep to myself."

"I think your teammates would like to see them."

"Not now," said Whiz. "Let's forget printing and stuff until we play some baseball."

"Deal," said E6.

They turned out the lights and left.

VINCENT CARY

Breadhurst Newts
Pitcher
Bats: R Throws: R
Ht: 5'5" Wt: 115 lbs.

He does okay.

"**W**here's Ace?" said Phoebe.

"Where's Diana?" said Wu.

"Where are the Twin Gloves of Glory?" said Dragon.

"They quit," said Whiz.

"All of them?" said Barney.

"Of course all of them," Delancey said. "Can you see one of them doing something separate from the other three?"

"How come they quit?" said Josiah, holding one shin guard. "Today's the last game. They could have played one more game."

E6 said, "Whiz and I saw them in town. They said they were sick of playing with a bunch of— well, with us."

The Newts all started speaking at once in a loud babble, railing at the four departed players, defending their own efforts, inventing interesting variations on the names *Ace, Diana, Max,* and *Marty.* Finally, Dragon spoke above the rest.

"I never much liked blazing, unhittable pitching, awesome batting power, and flashy, flawless fielding," he said. "I'd rather give the other team more of a chance." He looked around. "We like a *challenge,* right, mateys? Let's go out and nail these jerks to the wall!"

"You mean *blow them away,*" said Josiah.

"Yes," said E6 with a wide smile. "Blow them away, like nothing but *smoke.*"

The Newts took the field.